▶ ▶❙ 🔊 6:17 / 29:20

FGTeeV FAMILY BIOGRAPHY

8,857,752 VIEWS • 1 WEEK AGO   👍 283K 👎 8.5K → SHARE ＋ SAVE   •••

 FGTeeV
17.5M SUBSCRIBERS

Duddy, Moomy, Lexi, Mike, Chase, and Shawn are the stars of FGTeeV, one of the most popular family gaming YouTube channels in the world, with more than 17 million subscribers and 18 billion views. This family of six loves gaming, traveling, and spontaneous dance parties. To learn more, visit them on YouTube @FGTeeV.

4,120 COMMENTS

 Add a comment...

HARPERALLEY IS AN IMPRINT OF HARPERCOLLINS PUBLISHERS.

FGTEEV SAVES THE WORLD! COPYRIGHT © 2021 BY LAFFTER INC. ALL RIGHTS RESERVED. PRINTED IN THE UNITED STATES OF AMERICA. NO PART OF THIS BOOK MAY BE USED OR REPRODUCED IN ANY MANNER WHATSOEVER WITHOUT WRITTEN PERMISSION EXCEPT IN THE CASE OF BRIEF QUOTATIONS EMBODIED IN CRITICAL ARTICLES AND REVIEWS. FOR INFORMATION ADDRESS HARPERCOLLINS CHILDREN'S BOOKS, A DIVISION OF HARPERCOLLINS PUBLISHERS, 195 BROADWAY, NEW YORK, NY 10007. WWW.HARPERALLEY.COM

ISBN 978-0-06-304263-6

TYPOGRAPHY BY ERICA DE CHAVEZ. 21 22 23 24 25 MP 10 9 8 7 6 ❖ FIRST EDITION

SAVES THE WORLD!

By FGTeeV

Illustrated by Miguel Díaz Rivas

HARPER alley

An Imprint of HarperCollinsPublishers

CHARACTERS

DUDDY/ DUDSTER

This fun-loving dad has more achievements and power-ups than the best gamers in the world. But will all that be lost to history—and his greatest hero?

MOOMY

Moomy keeps the fun train from going off the rails, but she's also sweet, as you can see by her chocolate-chip freckle!

LEXI/LEXO

The boss of the children; the master strategist who takes control with the confidence of her gaming know-how.

MIKE/ MICKSTER

The second-in-command. Mike respects Lexi's rules . . . but that doesn't mean he always follows them.

CHASE/ DRIZZY

He's the fearless sharp-shooter of the family— even when he's drinking a slushie.

SHAWN/GHOST PUNCHER

Shawn is curious about everything, which sure keeps the family on its toes! He also thinks everything, no matter how dire, is hilarious!

THE MALL?!

WE HAVEN'T BEEN TO THE MALL IN **AGES**!

THERE'S A GAMING STORE THERE THAT MIGHT BE ABLE TO FIX IT.

THE MALL IS FOR **OLD PEOPLE**.

WHAT'S A "MALL"?

EW, WHAT'S THAT SMELL?

DON'T LOOK AT **ME**. I DIDN'T DO IT.

AHHH, IT SMELLS EXACTLY HOW IT DID WHEN WE WERE **TEENAGERS**.

YOU USED TO HANG OUT HERE WHEN YOU WERE TEENAGERS?

ALL THE COOL KIDS HUNG OUT AT THE MALL BACK IN THE DAY.

THEN WHAT WERE **THEY** DOING HERE?

THIS IS WHERE ME AND MOOMY HAD OUR **FIRST DATE**.

WE NEED A MALL DIRECTORY SO WE CAN FIND THE GAME STORE—

WELCOME TO THE SHADY ACRES MALL! DO YOU NEED ASSISTANCE?

AAHHH!

IT WOULDN'T MAKE SENSE TO DRIVE ALL THE WAY HOME JUST TO TURN AROUND AND COME BACK SO . . .

. . . WHY DON'T WE HANG OUT **HERE**?

. . .

I CAN'T STAY **HERE** IN THESE **PANTS**! WHAT IF I BUMP INTO SOMEONE I **KNOW**?

WHO ARE YOU GONNA BUMP INTO **HERE**—GRANDMA?

EVEN GRANDMA WOULD LAUGH AT HER PANTS.

YOU HAVE YOUR **BABYSITTING** MONEY, DON'T YOU? WE CAN SHOP TOGETHER!

SHAWN! IT WON'T BE A VERY FUN ANNIVERSARY FOR US IF WE HAVE TO REPORT A **MISSING CHILD**.

GET BACK HERE, MISTER!

MAYBE YOU'RE RIGHT— WE **SHOULD** STAY.

AND I'VE GOT A GREAT IDEA!

... MR. DUDDY IS THE BEST GAMER I'VE EVER SEEN! HIS AVATAR'S GOT A **FIVE STAR RATING**!

CECIL, ISN'T GRANNY WONDERING WHERE YOU ARE?

HE'S GOT ALL KINDS OF POWER-UPS AND BONUSES THAT NO ONE ELSE HAS! IF YOU LOSE THOSE ... YOU LOSE **HISTORY**!

AND YOU SHOULD CLEAN YOUR HARD DRIVE AFTERWARD 'CAUSE THAT STUFF COULD BE SOLD FOR THOUSANDS— NO, **MILLIONS**—ON THE INTERNET!

DON'T EVEN THINK ABOUT IT, BENNY.

DON'T THINK ABOUT **WHAT**?

POP!

BUMP!

HEY!

SHE'S SHOPPING FOR **NEW PANTS**.

IT'S, UH, **LAUNDRY DAY**. I HAD TO PUT ON AN **OLD** PAIR.

IF YOU'RE INTERESTED, G & N'S IS HAVING A SALE ON BELLA-BOTTOMS.

REALLY?!

THIS IS NO TIME TO POINT FINGERS— WE HAVE TO BUY A GIFT AND WE'RE RUNNING OUT OF TIME!

WALK FAST— LET'S GO!

AAAH!

NOW WHAT?

BRAIN FREEZE!

<HUFF HUFF> GET BACK . . . <HUFF>

DANG IT! I LOST THEM!

JAN'LL HAVE MY **BADGE** FOR THIS!

BUT DUDDY, WE DIDN'T DO ANYTHING WRONG! IT WAS OUR DOUBLES!

BUT YOURS DIDN'T HAVE A **CHOCOLATE CHIP FRECKLE** LIKE YOU. SO THEY WEREN'T **DOUBLES**—

—THEY WERE OUR **GAME AVATARS**!

I'D KNOW THAT BARK **ANYWHERE**! IT'S **OREO**!

STAFF

ARF! ARF! ARF!

OREO, OUR VIDEO GAME AVATARS CAME TO LIFE AND THEY'RE IN THE MALL!

YES, I KNOW. **I JUST SAID THAT.**

OUT OF THE WAY!

IT'S AN EMERGENCY!

MIKE...!

MIKE, WATCH OUT!

SKREET!

WHAT'S WRONG WITH YOU? DON'T YOU KNOW AN AMERICAN HERO WHEN YOU SEE ONE?

I AM IN CONTROL OF THIS GAME NOW, AND I HAVE A **MISSION** FOR YOU!

I WANT YOU TO FOLLOW THE TWO FUGITIVES ON THOSE ANIMALS—

—AND **DESTROY** THEM.

THE CONTROLLER THAT SHALL NOT BE TOUCHED . . .

IT HAS A FUNKY GLITCH . . .

HAVE TO SAVE THE KIDS! SAVE THE FAMILY!

BUT . . . BUT . . . YOU AND DAD ALWAYS KNOW WHAT TO DO!

SHE'S RIGHT, MOOMY— WE **DO**.

SO WHAT IF WE'RE HEAVILY OUTNUMBERED . . .

SO WHAT IF WE'RE UP AGAINST POWERED-UP VERSIONS OF OURSELVES—AND THE GREATEST MILITARY MIND EVER PROGRAMMED . . .

WE'LL JUST HAVE TO **WING** IT! LET'S GO!

POOR DUDDZ!

DON'T WORRY—THE AVATAR'S ONLY SO STRONG BECAUSE DUDDY'S SUCH A GREAT GAMER—HE'LL FIGURE THIS OUT!

HUH? WHERE DID YOU GET **THAT**?

YES! I'M **BACK IN THE GAME!**